Middleton Public Library
7425 Hubbard Ave
Middleton, WI 53562

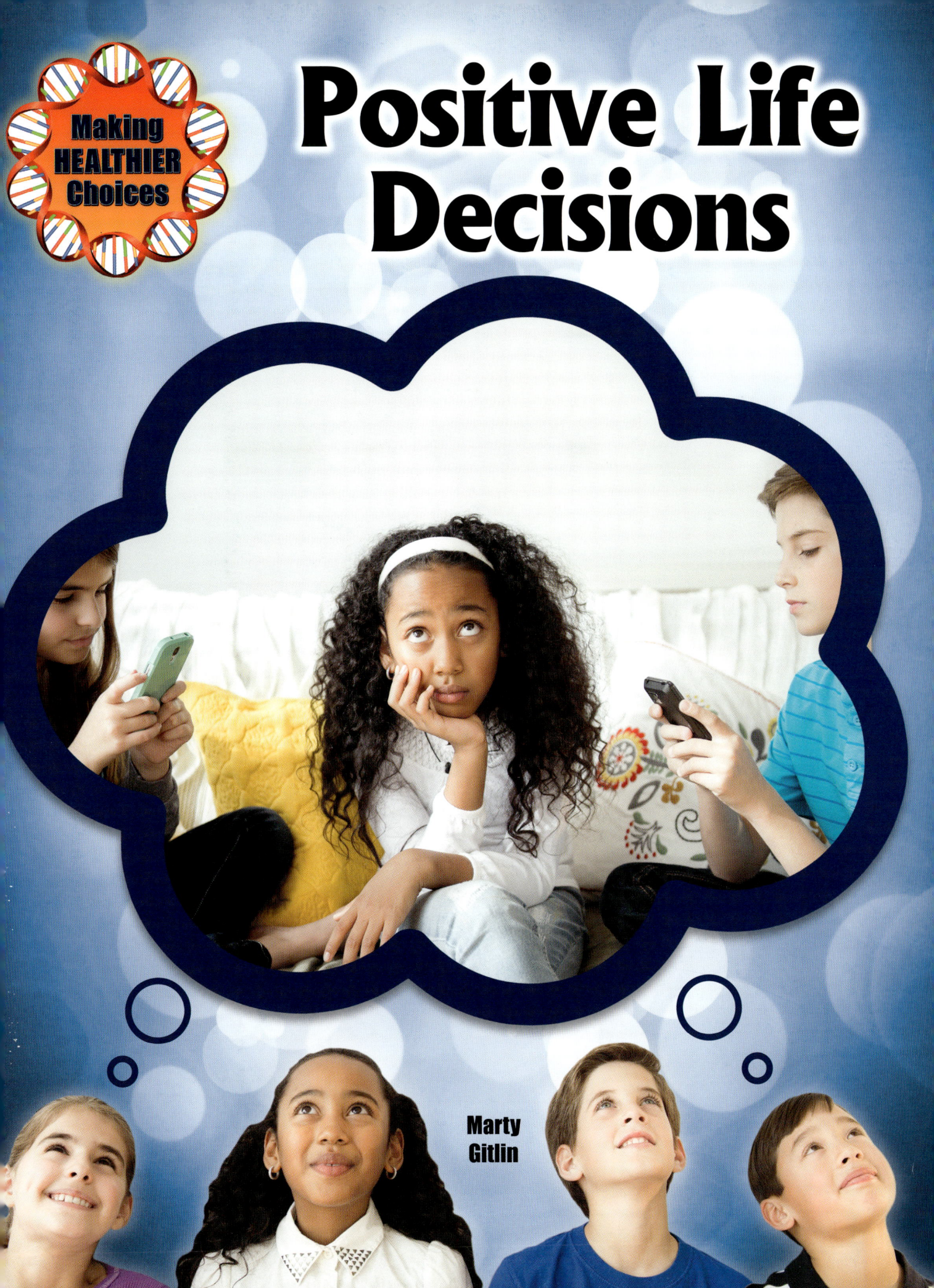

Mitchell Lane

PUBLISHERS
2001 SW 31st Avenue
Hallandale, FL 33009
www.mitchelllane.com

Copyright © 2019 by Mitchell Lane Publishers. All rights reserved. No part of this book may be reproduced without written permission from the publisher. Printed and bound in the United States of America.

First Edition, 2019
Designer: Sharon Beck
Editor: Jim Whiting

Library of Congress Cataloging-in-Publication Data
Names: Gitlin, Marty, author.
Title: Positive life decisions / by Marty Gitlin.
Description: Hallandale, FL : Mitchell Lane Publishers, [2019] | Series: Making healthier choices | Includes bibliographical references and index.
Identifiers: LCCN 2018003186 | ISBN 9781680202762 (library bound) | ISBN 9781680202779
Subjects: LCSH: Decision making in children—Juvenile literature. | Decision making—Juvenile literature. | Conduct of life—Juvenile literature.
Classification: LCC BF723.D34 G58 2018 | DDC 155.4/1383—dc23
LC record available at https://lccn.loc.gov/2018003186

eBook ISBN: 978-1-68020-277-9

PHOTO CREDITS: Cover and interior art—JGI/Jamie Grill/Getty Images, Yuri_Arcurs/Getty Images, AlonzoDesign/Getty Images, A-R-T-U-R/Getty Images; cover, p. 1—JGI/Jamie Grill/Getty Images; amtitus/Getty Images, Neustockimages/Getty Images; p. 5—Creative-Family/Getty Images, Monkey Business Images/Getty Images; p. 6—LittleBee80/Getty Images; p. 9—Digital Vision/Getty Images, PeopleImages/Getty Images; p. 11—KatarzynaBialasiewicz/Getty Images; p. 13—Jamie Grill Photography/Getty Images; p. 15—Wavebreakmedia/Getty Images, Jose Girarte/Getty Images; p. 17—Hill Street Studios/Getty Images; p. 18—Rubberball/Nicole Hill/Getty Images; p. 19—Niedring/Drentwett/Getty Images; p. 21—SLP_London/Getty Images, triocean/Getty Images; p. 22—Jennierae Gonzalez/EyeEm/Getty Images; p. 24—JGI/Jamie Grill/Getty Images; p. 25—DougSchneiderPhoto/Getty Images; p. 27—Photodisc/Getty Images, Stockbyte/Getty Images; p. 29—Nastia11/Getty Images.

Contents

Chapter 1 ◆ The First Steps 4

Chapter 2 ◆ Doing the Right Thing 8

Chapter 3 ◆ Decisions, Decisions, Decisions 14

Chapter 4 ◆ Making Tougher Choices 20

Chapter 5 ◆ It Is Not All About You 26

Find Out More 30
Works Consulted 30
Index 32

CHAPTER 1
The First Steps

Jim Taylor is a doctor. Not the kind of doctor who listens to your heartbeat, gives you shots, or removes your tonsils. Taylor is a doctor of the mind. He studies how children think.

Taylor often speaks with groups of kids. He asks them if they have ever done something stupid. And they always react the same way. They all raise their hands.

Then the doctor asks them why they did stupid things. Why did they make those poor decisions? The kids state some or all of the following reasons:

- I did not stop to think.
- It seemed like fun at the time.
- I was bored.
- My friends put pressure on me.
- I did not consider what would happen.

Almost always the children say they regret doing stupid things. But Dr. Taylor thinks that dumb decisions help kids.

Why? Because they make children wiser. They learn from their mistakes. And they make better decisions later in life.

You can't do your homework or study for a test when you are distracted by texting with your friends. Decide to turn your phone off or put it in another room and ignore it until you're finished.

Every decision is a fork in the road. Quite often, there is a right road and a wrong road. Many times, the wrong road looks more exciting and fun. It does not invite thought. You might want to jump right on it.

The right road might appear boring. But it is the smart path to take.

Chapter 1

Deciding to have the apple instead of the candy is a good decision.

Most decisions you make are small ones. Should I help wash the dishes or run outside and play? Should I play a video game or do my homework? Should I eat candy or some fruit before bed? But even here, there is usually a right and a wrong choice.

It would be easy to let someone else wash the dishes. It would allow you to do something more fun. But helping shows that you care about others. And it builds a strong work ethic.

You would rather play a video game than do homework. But you know that the homework is more important. It will make you smarter. And it will better prepare you for school the next day.

Candy or fruit? You know the right answer. Sugary candy may keep you awake. It is bad for your teeth. Foods like oranges and cherries help you sleep. And they are good for your body.

Some decisions require time and thought. But candy or fruit? That is a simple choice. You are old enough to know better. But you are still tempted to unwrap that candy. You must simply be strong enough to grab the fruit instead.

An episode of an old TV show called *Leave It to Beaver* gives an example. Its main character was a kid named Beaver Cleaver. Beaver and his buddies all bought ugly sweatshirts. The sweatshirts featured pictures of goofy monsters. The monster on Beaver's sweatshirt had three eyeballs!

The kids agreed to wear them to school the next day. Beaver's parents ordered him not to wear his. So he snuck it out of the house. When he was out of his parents' sight, he put on the shirt and wore it to school.

There was one problem. None of his friends wore their monster shirts. Beaver was the only one wearing one. He was embarrassed. All the kids laughed at him. He got in trouble with the school. And he lost the trust of his parents when they found out that he had disobeyed them.

They punished Beaver. He was grounded for the weekend. But his father also gave him a bit of wonderful advice. "Wrong is wrong even if everyone says it's right," he told his son. "And right is right even if everyone else says it's wrong."

That is true. You should always figure out the wise choice. Weigh what is right and what is wrong. You can do this even for small decisions such as eating fruit instead of candy.

Get into the habit of doing what you know is best. Then it is easier to make the right decisions as time goes on. That is important. After all, you will be making bigger decisions as you get older.

> **Get into the habit of doing what you know is best. Then it is easier to make the right decisions as time goes on. That is important.**

CHAPTER 2
Doing the Right Thing

You make easy decisions every day. In fact, they are so easy that you give them little thought. What cereal do you want for breakfast? Which socks should you wear to school? What video game would you like to play when you get home?

Some decisions are a bit tougher. They require more thinking. Who should you invite to your birthday party? What subject should you choose for your science report?

Other life choices can be very hard. They often involve others. Should you tell on your brother for breaking a vase? Should you stand and watch as a classmate is bullied?

Parents make most decisions for little children. They pick out clothes for their youngsters to wear. They choose everything their kids eat. As you grow, you make more of your own decisions. And these decisions often become harder as you get older.

Making decisions can lead to good or bad results. Learning to make right choices is an important step in maturing. Experts cite four basic steps to making good decisions.

The first step is to define the problem. For example, let's say your parents have told you

As you get older, you won't have to rely on your parents to pick out what to wear.

to play some sports this summer. But you can only pick two. That is an easy problem to define. Your parents have limited you to two sports. Which ones will you choose?

The second step is to consider your choices. You must choose among soccer,

Chapter 2

Not all decisions are easy. Some are more complicated. In cases like those, it's best to seek help. It is often best to get advice from adults you trust.

softball, tennis, and basketball. You like all of them. How can you narrow the choices?

The third step is to assess each one of them. Of these four, basketball is your favorite. But it can be played indoors. You can wait until winter when the weather is cold and often rainy.

You enjoy tennis. But none of your friends play tennis. It will be hard to find someone to practice with.

You can join leagues for soccer and softball. The best time to play these sports is during the summer.

The fourth and final step is to actually make the decision, based on the assessments you made in step three. You choose to play soccer and softball.

You have thought things out well! Be proud that you reasoned it out by yourself. Your choices are based on logic and interest. And have fun!

Not all decisions are easy. Some are more complicated. In cases like those, it's best to seek help. It is often best to get advice from adults you trust.

Do you have an issue in class? Ask your teacher about it.

Do you have a problem at home? Talk it over with your parents.

Do you have a personal issue? Discuss it with a school counselor or parent.

Maybe you feel another kid, such as a good friend or one of your siblings, would better understand. If so, confide in them.

The views of people you trust can help. Consider their opinions. Then make the decision by yourself. That is part of growing up.

Doing the Right Thing

If you need help or advice about a decision you have to make, you can talk to your school counselor.

11

Chapter 2

> **Perhaps your decision turns out to be wrong. Do not be angry with yourself. Just learn from it. Try to make a better choice next time. And be proud that you followed all the right steps when you made the decision.**

So is making mistakes. Perhaps your decision turns out to be wrong. Do not be angry with yourself. Just learn from it. Try to make a better choice next time. And be proud that you followed all the right steps when you made the decision.

You can even practice making decisions. It is fun. Pretend you are faced with a problem. What choices would you make? Could you solve it by yourself? Or would you need help? Who would you ask for advice?

Let's say your teacher gave you an A on a test. But it was a mistake. Somehow, your teacher switched your grades by accident with a classmate. The perfect grade belonged to him. He got your C-plus.

Do you say nothing and take the A? You can sure use that great grade! Do you wait to see if your classmate notices? Or do you tell your teacher right away?

It is always best to tell the truth. You should inform the teacher of her error. She would appreciate your honesty. So would your classmate. And you would respect yourself.

Think of other situations that would require a decision. Talk them over with your parents. Learn if the choice they would make is different than yours.

You never know. A situation like that could arise for real someday. And even if it does not? Pretending it does can be fun. It can also be a great life lesson.

Doing the Right Thing

Your classmate is an A student and studied hours for the test. You didn't study as much as you should have, and he ended up with the C+ you got on your test. He is disappointed. Put yourself in his shoes and chose to be honest.

CHAPTER 3
Decisions, Decisions, Decisions

You are sitting in your classroom. The music teacher walks in. She has a violin in her hands. And a big smile on her face.

She says that a very generous person just donated four violins to the school. She does not want them to go to waste.

"Who wants to take violin lessons?" she asks. Two kids raise their hands right away. You are tempted to join them. But you do not want to rush into anything. You ask the music teacher for time to decide.

"That is fine," she says. "But no later than tomorrow. I only have two violins left. And others might also be interested."

How do you choose? You only have one day. This is a big decision. It is best to take it one step at a time.

That means asking yourself questions. And listing the good and bad results. You return home and list the following thoughts:

Why would I want violin lessons?
- My best friend raised his hand. I can take lessons with him.
- I have always wanted a musical talent.

14

Is the violin a right choice for you?

- My parents have suggested that I learn how to play a musical instrument.
- I enjoy the sound of the violin.

CHAPTER 3

Why should I reject the offer?
- It would take away from the time I spend at soccer practice.
- I like the piano better.
- I would have to practice an hour a day.
- I hear that the music teacher is strict and mean.

What are my options?
- Agree to take violin lessons.
- Ask my parents if I can take piano lessons instead.
- Forget music for now and maintain the same schedule of my other activities.

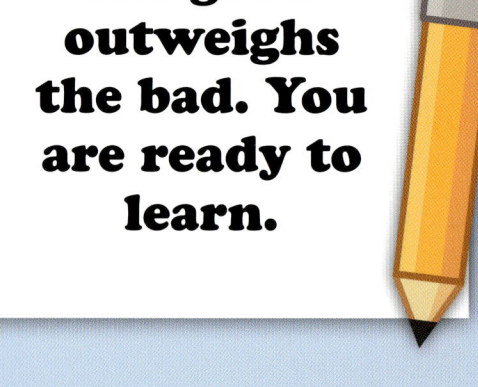

How would it change my life?
- I would have less time to do homework.
- I would miss the bus after school and need a ride home.
- I would learn a new skill that I could keep forever.
- It would make me feel good about myself.

After looking over all the items on your list, you decide that the good outweighs the bad. You are ready to learn.

You talk to your friend and both sets of parents. They can arrange a carpool. It would get you home from school. Your mom says you can take piano lessons if you do not like the violin. You figure out a time for soccer and homework.

After looking over all the items on your list, you decide that the good outweighs the bad. You are ready to learn. You tell your music teacher to hand over a violin. And after you have been taking lessons for a while, you realize that she is not strict and mean after all. She is as nice as can be.

Decisions, Decisions, Decisions

Taking violin lessons with your friends.

Chapter 3

You will fight the battle between right and wrong for your entire life. It is important to start out on the right path.

The decision-making process worked! You made a wise choice. You realize that is very important. You know bigger decisions await you as you get older. They might affect you for the rest of your life.

Some will be battles between right and wrong. They will test your ability to avoid temptation.

Maybe you have already been tested. The temptation to cheat in school is one example.

Perhaps you sit behind a straight-A student in class. You can see every quiz answer on her paper. You studied for the quiz at home. But you are not sure how to answer every question.

Looking at your classmate's answers on a quiz is cheating.

Decisions, Decisions, Decisions

Maybe you wrote answers on a cheat sheet. This is also being dishonest.

You look at your teacher. She is not paying attention. It would be so easy to sneak a peek at the straight-A student's answers. You are sure they are correct.

What do you do? You might get a C if you do not cheat. You could get an A if you do. But you will not have earned it.

You must make a split-second decision. You know the answer in your heart and mind. It is a matter of right and wrong. You should keep your eyes on your own paper. Do the best you can. Turn in an honest quiz. And live with the grade you get.

It is better to feel good about yourself. Cheaters know that they don't really achieve anything. It is often harder to be honest. And cheating can become a habit. Cheat once and it becomes easier the next time. But you will live in fear of getting caught.

You will fight the battle between right and wrong for your entire life. It is important to start out on the right path.

CHAPTER 4
Making Tougher Choices

You are worried about your older brother. He is in high school. He walks home every day. His path takes him past some of his classmates on a street corner. They are all "popular" kids. And they always stand around smoking cigarettes after school.

Your brother knows the dangers of smoking. He realizes it causes cancer and many other health problems. He has always passed right by the other students. But last week he stopped. He wanted to be popular too.

They offered him a cigarette. He accepted. Now he smokes with them every day. He coughs a lot at home. He gets winded playing soccer with you. But he likes his new friends. He even began dating one of them.

You will probably be faced with the same choice when you go to high school. Kids have been smoking on that street corner for many years. Perhaps you will be tempted.

The decision should be easy. You know smoking is terrible. You feel it has done your brother much more harm than good.

How do you avoid that trap? Will you be strong enough to say no? You might feel it is

Smoking is bad for your health. Don't let peer pressure make you try it.

a choice between your health and being popular. This is when making positive life decisions gets harder.

The answer is easy: Just be yourself. Do not decide based on how others might judge you. Those who would only befriend you if you smoke with them are not worthy of your friendship.

Chapter 4

Kids often make snap decisions. They act without thinking. Are you one of them? Then you need to stop and think for a few seconds. What would the result be of your actions? Why would you want to do this?

Why do kids sometimes do wrong things? Is it peer pressure? Kids must often choose between doing what is right or what could make them popular. Studies have shown that kids often choose what they believe will make them popular.

Is it something that might feel good for the moment? Kids often do not think about the long-term results of their choices. So they make the wrong decision. They regret it later.

You know that. You think back to the night when you drank a bottle of soda pop and ate candy just before bedtime. They sure tasted good! But you could not fall asleep. You woke up tired. You nearly nodded off in class. You enjoyed the soda and candy for a few minutes. That was followed by a night and a day of misery.

Eating a lot of candy is not good for you. If you eat it before you go to bed, you'll most likely regret it.

How do you become a great decision-maker? The best way is to consider every option. Then think about the likely results.

Playing a game of "What If?" can provide great practice. How about this one?

"What If?" your best friend runs away from home. He asks you to hide him in your house. "Don't tell my parents," he says.

Possible Decision 1: You hide your friend in your basement.
Possible Outcomes:
- His parents are sick with worry. They are angry with you when they find out that you let him hide with you.
- Your parents punish you.
- Your friend might not solve whatever problem he had at home.

Possible Decision 2: Inform his parents.
Possible Outcomes:
- You lose your friendship.
- Your friend tells your classmates that you are a fink.
- His parents thank you for being honest and caring about their son.

Possible Decision 3: Talk it over with your parents.
Possible Outcomes:
- Your parents get angry. They send your friend home.
- They call his parents and tell them to pick him up.
- They give you one hour to convince your friend to go home.

23

Chapter 4

Making the wrong choices has consequences. Your parents may discipline or punish you, but it's only because they care. They want you to make the right decisions.

Possible Decision 4: Your friend tells you why he ran away. You try to convince him to return home. You tell him he should solve his issues with his parents.

Possible Outcomes:

- Your friend refuses to speak with you about it.
- He tells you why he ran away, but will not go home.
- You succeed in convincing him to go home. He says he will work out his problems.
- Your parents and his parents thank you.

There is no perfect decision. You do know your friend cannot stay with you forever. The best you can do is pick the option you think is best.

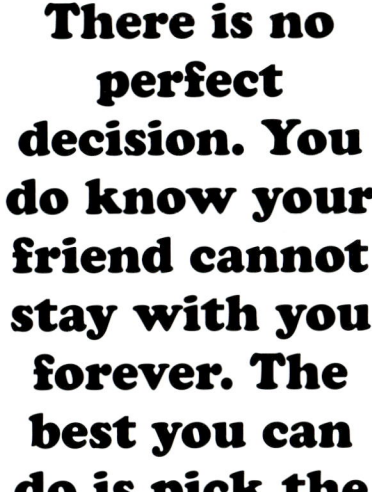

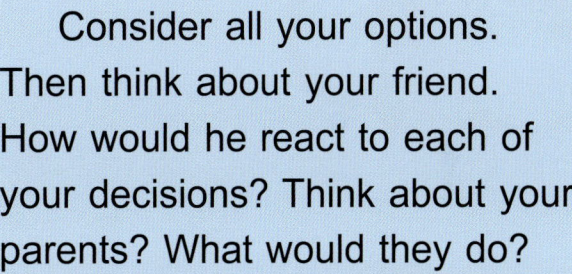

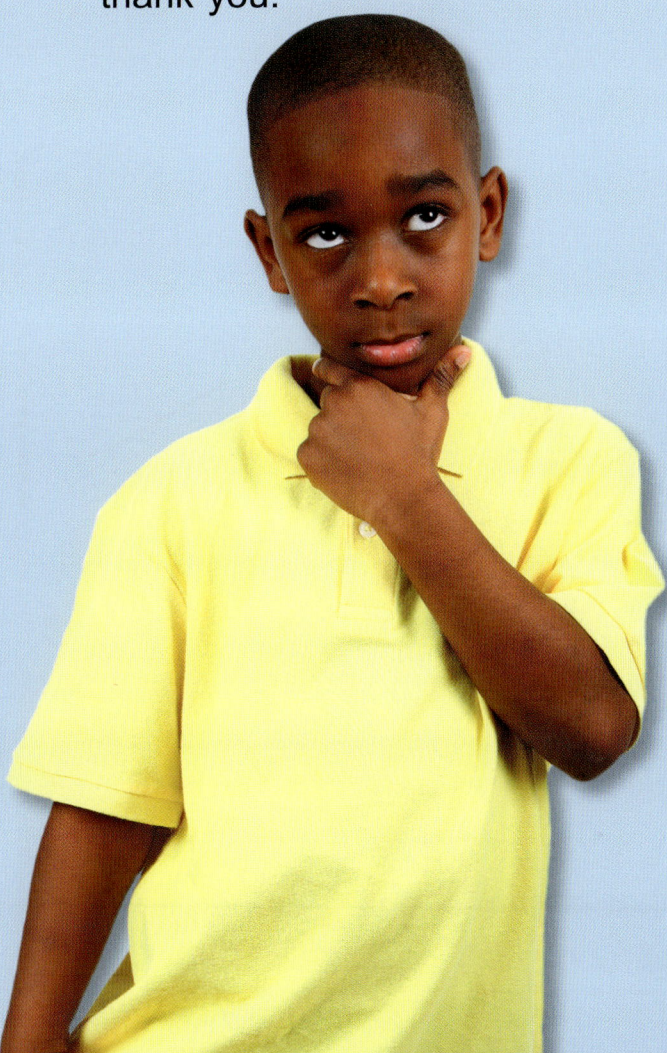

Consider all your options. Then think about your friend. How would he react to each of your decisions? Think about your parents? What would they do?

There is no perfect decision. You do know your friend cannot stay with you forever. The best you can do is pick the option you think is best.

And if you do that in real life? You will be a better person.

CHAPTER 5
It Is Not All About You

Kids often don't think about how their actions affect others. For example, let's say that your sister got a new video game for her birthday. You are mad. It is the one you wanted for your birthday. You even asked your parents for it. But they bought you a lousy shirt instead.

Your anger grows. Then you come up with a plan. You will steal the game and play it in your room. You will turn it off if you hear anyone coming.

Your sister will think she misplaced it. Later on, you can pretend you found it and give it back to her. You will be a hero.

There is almost no way of getting caught. And so what if you do? You can just claim you borrowed the game.

It seems like a perfect plan. But your thinking does not go beyond the plan. You do not think about if it is right or wrong. You are mad at your parents. Yet you are stealing from your sister. She loves that game. And now she will be without it.

It does not matter that you can get away with it. What is right is right. And what is wrong is wrong.

26

It is wrong to take something that belongs to your sibling without asking. Doing so is stealing and trying to cover it up with a plan is lying.

Chapter 5

> **You have learned that many of the choices you make affect others as well. So you need to think about friends and family members. How are they affected by a decision you make?**

You are being selfish. Your sister will be upset. She will break into tears. She will think she lost the game. She will blame herself. But she has done nothing wrong.

Your parents will be mad at your sister. They will also think she lost it. They might even punish her for being careless.

You love your sister. But you are taking out your anger toward your parents on her. Stealing the game is a terrible idea. You know that.

You wait until you calm down. Then you come up with a better plan. You calmly ask your parents why they did not buy the game for you. You let them know you are upset.

Great decision! You are being honest instead of sneaky. You are being thoughtful toward your sister. You are respecting your parents. And you will feel better about yourself.

You have learned that many of the choices you make affect others as well. So you need to think about friends and family members. How are they affected by a decision you make? Now that thought enters your mind every time you make a decision. It has become a wonderful habit.

Do the right thing for yourself and for others. It could be your sister or a parent or a friend. Even a total stranger.

Say you find a purse on the ground. It has a lot of money in it. There is nothing in it to identify the owner.

You can keep the money. You do not even have to tell anyone. Or you can turn the purse in to the police. That may give the person who

It Is Not All About You

You find a wallet with a lot of money in it. The right thing to do is give it to your parents. If there's no identification, they can turn it over to the police. The owner will be glad to have it back.

lost it a chance to identify it. It would be easy to pocket the cash. Or you could leave the purse where you found it.

But you know the right decision in your heart and mind. You do not know the person who lost the purse. But you are thinking about her. You are sure she is upset.

You do not hesitate. It takes just a few seconds to decide. You tell your parents to drive you to the police station. You are going to turn in the purse.

Maybe it will not be claimed. Then you can keep the money. But you hope not. You prefer that the rightful owner claims it.

When you were younger, you might have kept the money. But now you think about others. You are making the right choices. You are proving that you care about people. Even people you never met.

You are now an honest, mature human being. You should be proud of yourself!

FIND OUT MORE

Books

Engelhardt, Lisa O. *Making Good Choices: A Book About Right and Wrong.* Meinrad, IN: Abbey Press, 2013.

George, Elizabeth. A *Girl's Guide to Making Really Good Choices.* Eugene, OR: Harvest House Publishers, 2013.

George, Jim. *A Boy's Guide to Making Really Good Choices.* Eugene, OR: Harvest House Publishers, 2013.

Smith, Bryan. *What Were You Thinking? Learning to Control Your Impulses*. Baltimore, MD: Brookes Publishing, 2016.

Websites

Kids Matter: About Good Decision-Making
https://www.kidsmatter.edu.au/families/about-behaviour/making-decisions/learning-make-good-decisions-and-solve-problems

Chiesman: Good Choice, Bad Choice
http://www.chiesman.org/pdfs/rcccp1/GoodChoiceBadChoice.pdf

Mom.me: Fun activities to teach children about decision-making skills
https://mom.me/kids/4887-fun-activities-teach-children-about-decision-making-skills/

WORKS CONSULTED

"5 reasons to let children make their own decisions." Mom it Forward, May 30, 2017. http://momitforward.com/5-reasons-let-children-make-their-own-decisions/

"Leave It to Beaver – S05E35 – Sweatshirt Monsters." Dailymotion.com https://www.dailymotion.com/video/x59w87d

Morgan, Linda. "Raising good decision makers: Helping kids learn to make decisions." Parent Map, September 28, 2011. https://www.parentmap.com/article/helping-kids-learn-to-make-decisions

Taylor, Dr. Jim. "Raising Good Decision Makers." *Huffington Post*, November 17, 2011. https://www.huffingtonpost.com/dr-jim-taylor/teaching-decision-making_b_825414.html

Walker, Carson. "Are you teaching kids how to make good decisions? Here's how to be sure." A Fine Parent. https://afineparent.com/strong-kids/how-to-make-good-decisions.html

"What to do—making decisions." Kids' Health, Women's and Children's Health Network. http://www.cyh.com/HealthTopics/HealthTopicDetailsKids.aspx?p=335&np=287&id=2975

INDEX

boredom   4, 5
bullying   8
cheating   18-19
classmates   8, 12, 13, 18, 20, 23
clothing   8
counselors   10
food   6-7, 22
friendship   4, 7, 10, 14, 16, 17, 20, 21, 23, 25, 28
homework   5, 6, 16
Leave it to Beaver   7
mistakes   4, 12
parents   8-9, 10, 12, 15, 16, 23, 24, 25, 26, 28, 29

peer pressure   4, 21, 22
popularity   20, 21, 22
punishment   7, 23, 24, 28
school   6, 7, 8, 14, 16, 18, 20
smoking   20, 21
sports   9-10
stealing   26-28
Taylor, Dr. Jim   4
teachers   10, 12, 14, 16, 19
temptations   18
tests   5, 12, 13, 18, 19
video games   6, 8, 26
violin   14, 15, 16, 17